THE MYSTE OF THE JADE PRINCESS

MARILYN GRANBECK

This book is dedicated to Kim Stoepfel

Illustrations by Michael Garland

Copyright © 1989, 1979 by Marilyn Granbeck.
All rights reserved. Published by Scholastic Inc.
SPRINT and SPRINT BOOKS are trademarks of Scholastic Inc.
Printed in the U.S.A.
ISBN 0-590-35201-6

8 9 10   31   03 02 01 00 99

CHAPTER 1

Sue Lee and Jenny Fong hurried along Sun Street.

"It's only a few days until the New Year's celebration," Sue said. Chinese New Year was an exciting time, with parades, dances, and fireworks. Sue liked it better than any other time of the year.

"This year's parade is going to be the best one ever," Jenny said.

Sue sighed. "I wish I were in it instead of just watching." Sue's brother Jimmy was in the parade. He was going to help carry the big paper dragon. The dragon was part of the holiday parade. It was not too heavy, but it took 10 people to hold its tail. Together, they made it dance along the street.

Jenny did not care about being in the parade. She was happy to be in the Girls' Club's special program of Chinese dances. Sue's grandmother was letting them wear beautiful old Chinese robes from her trunk. Jenny's was red, with a dragon stitched in gold thread on the back. Sue's was yellow, with trees and hills sewn in silver and blue. Every day after school, Sue and Jenny went to the club to practice. They were on their way there now.

"Let's walk past Mr. Chin's shop and see the Jade Princess," Sue said.

Mr. Chin and his daughter Ruth owned a gift shop on Lotus Street. Mr. Chin liked to talk about when he lived in China, long ago. Even more, he liked to talk about what a good place Chinatown was. Mr. Chin was the leader of the Chinatown Men's Club. The club helped new families settle in Chinatown. It also put on the New Year's parade. Ruth helped out at the Girls' Club. She taught the Chinese dances. And she helped the girls get their costumes ready for the program.

Every year in honor of the celebration, Mr. Chin put a jade statue in the window of his shop. The green stone figure of a woman was about 10 inches tall. Her head was bowed. Her face was partly hidden behind a fan. Everyone called it the Jade Princess.

Mr. Chin had brought the statue from China a long time ago. He said it was the Princess of Happiness. Ruth had let Jenny and Sue hold the Princess. The green stone was smooth and cool. The Princess seemed to smile behind her fan. Ruth had told them that the statue had belonged to the Chin family for many years. Her father had been offered a lot of money for it. But he would not sell. He said as long as the

Jade Princess smiled on Chinatown, the people would be happy.

Sue and Jenny turned the corner onto Lotus Street. The girls knew that in a few days the street would have a holiday look. Paper lanterns and flowers would be hung everywhere. On the door of each shop, lettuce and folded dollar bills would be tied on strings. These were gifts for the dragon. The

paper dragon would dance from shop to shop.
Then people would give it their gifts. The
dragon chased away bad spirits.

Sue and Jenny saw Mr. Chin in the doorway
of his shop. He was talking to two men. They
seemed angry. Mr. Chin was angry too. He
was trying to get the men out of his shop.

The short fat man yelled at him. "You are not
being very smart, Chin!"

9

The tall, skinny man shook his fist. "You will be sorry if you do not listen to us!"

Mr. Chin shook his head. "Never!" he said. "I will not do it!"

The short man said something Sue and Jenny did not hear. Then Mr. Chin pushed away the skinny man and slammed the door. The fat man looked angry enough to break the door down, but he turned away. The two of them got into a blue car at the curb. Sue and Jenny watched the car drive away.

"I wonder what they want Mr. Chin to do," Jenny said.

"I don't know," Sue said. "But Mr. Chin does not look happy about it. I don't think he likes those two men."

The car went past the girls and around the corner. The two men still looked angry. Then they were gone.

Sue and Jenny walked up to the store. Mr. Chin had pulled down the shade behind the door. A sign that said CLOSED was hanging on the door.

That surprised Sue and Jenny. It was not like Mr. Chin to close the shop so early. They looked in the window where the Jade Princess was supposed to be. They saw the carved ivory box with the black velvet lining. But it was empty. The Jade Princess was gone!

CHAPTER 2

The two girls looked at each other. Where was the Jade Princess?

"Mr. Chin always keeps the Jade Princess in the window for the New Year," Sue said. She stared at the empty box. "Why isn't it here now?"

"Maybe he hasn't put it out yet," Jenny said.

Sue shook her head. "The box is there." It was a special box that Mr. Chin always kept the statue in.

Sue and Jenny peered through the window. The shop was dark and looked empty. Mr. Chin was not behind the counter. He wasn't near any of the shelves that held carvings, dishes, and other beautifully made things.

Sue went to the door and turned the knob. It was locked.

"This is very strange," she said. "Maybe he's in the back of the store."

"Maybe he had to go shopping or to the bank," Jenny said. She was trying to find a reason for Mr. Chin's strange action. "Or maybe he went to the Men's Club to work on the parade."

"He didn't come out. We were right here in

front of the shop. We would have seen him,"
Sue said.

"Maybe he went out the back door," Jenny
said.

The back door opened onto an alley. Mr.
Chin and Ruth did not use it often. He could
have gone out that way, but Sue did not think
so. She still thought it was very odd for Mr.
Chin to lock up the store so early. He was here

only a few minutes ago with two men. Did he leave the shop because of them? Sue peered anxiously through the glass again. The shop was the same as it always was, except that Mr. Chin and the Jade Princess were not there.

"We're going to be late for practice if we don't hurry," Jenny said.

Sue gave one last look inside the shop. Then the two girls hurried toward the club.

The club room was nearly full. Girls were laughing and talking happily. Chinese music was playing on a record player. Ruth Chin clapped her hands and told the girls to form a line. The dance practice was about to begin. She smiled warmly and waved when she saw Sue and Jenny.

Sue wanted to ask her about the Jade Princess, but Ruth was too busy to talk now. Sue and Jenny put down their books and sweaters and took their places in the line. The music started again. The girls began to dance.

Ruth was a very good dancer. She was a very good teacher too. She showed the girls how to dance gracefully and how to move their hands to tell the story of the dance. The dance always made Sue think of China, where her parents and grandparents had lived. The soft music of bells, flutes, and harps seemed to come from another place and another time.

Sue forgot about the missing jade statue. During the weeks of practice, she had come to love the music that was part of China's history. She loved the exotic costumes and the wonderful stories Mr. Chin told too. For a while she even forgot about wanting to be in the grand parade. She was glad to be dancing in the program for the holiday celebration.

When the practice was over Sue and Jenny

stayed after the other girls left. Then Sue asked Ruth, "Why did your father take the Jade Princess out of the shop window?"

Ruth looked very surprised. "He wouldn't do that," she said.

"Jenny and I walked past the shop on our way from school. The Princess isn't in the window." Sue wondered if she should tell Ruth about the two men who were arguing with Mr. Chin.

Ruth looked puzzled for a moment, then she smiled. "I don't know why he did it, but I'm sure he had a good reason. Perhaps he wanted to polish the statue or clean the window. I'm sure he has put the Princess back by now."

Ruth picked up her coat and purse. "It's getting late. I'll see you two tomorrow. Please try to be on time. We have only two more days to practice before the New Year." She let the girls out and began to lock up the club rooms.

Sue and Jenny walked down Lotus Street on the way home. Sue hoped Ruth was right. She hoped the Jade Princess was back in the shop window. But as they neared the shop, they saw it was still dark.

The window was empty. There was no sign of the lovely Jade Princess or of Mr. Chin.

CHAPTER 3

Sue and Jenny were still staring at the empty window when Ruth Chin came up the street. She was surprised to see them at the shop. She was more surprised to see the empty box in the window. She unlocked the door and hurried inside.

"Father? Father?" she called out. She went through the shop. She looked behind the counter and around the tables. She even looked behind a tall rice paper screen painted with pictures. Finally she pushed aside the thick curtain that covered the doorway to the back room.

"Father!" she cried.

Sue and Jenny rushed into the room. Ruth was kneeling beside her father. Mr. Chin lay on the floor. His hands and feet were tied with rope. A heavy cloth covered his mouth. He looked pale and scared.

Quickly Sue helped Ruth untie the knots in the rope. They took the gag off Mr. Chin's mouth. Jenny ran to the sink and got a glass of water. Ruth put her arm around her father and helped him sit up. He looked dazed as he drank the water.

"What happened?" Ruth wanted to know. She looked worried.

"Were you robbed?" Sue asked.

"We ought to call the police," Jenny said.

The old man looked up quickly. "Don't do that. Nothing has been stolen."

"The Jade Princess is gone," Jenny said.

Mr. Chin shook his head. His white beard brushed against the silk robe he wore. "Nothing has been stolen," he repeated. His voice was weak and his hands were shaky.

Ruth helped him get up and led him to a chair. He sat looking at his hands as he rubbed them together. "Do not call the police," he insisted.

"But someone tied you up!" Sue said. And Jenny was right—the Jade Princess *was* gone. If it wasn't stolen, where was it? There had to be a robber.

Mr. Chin took a deep breath and looked at the girls. "You must not call the police. And you must not tell anyone what you saw here today."

There was a puzzled look on Ruth's face as she watched her father. She put a hand on his shoulder.

"Are you sure you're all right, Father?"

He did not look all right, but he nodded. "I'm tired, that's all."

Ruth did not ask him any more questions. She turned to Sue and Jenny. "My father needs to rest. I'll take him home. Thank you for helping."

Sue did not understand what was going on. Even if Mr. Chin did not want to talk about it, something was certainly wrong. Sue was sure it had to do with the missing jade statue and the two men they had seen earlier. But she did not want to make more trouble for Mr. Chin and Ruth.

"We won't say anything," Sue promised. "I hope you feel better soon, Mr. Chin."

The old man smiled. "Thank you."

Sue and Jenny said good-bye and left the shop. Outside, they stopped to look at the empty box in the window. It seemed very strange not to see the Jade Princess there.

Sue frowned. "No matter what Mr. Chin says, I think the Jade Princess has been stolen. Why do you think he doesn't want to talk about it?"

"I don't know," Jenny said. She was not sure the statue had actually been stolen. If it had been, Mr. Chin would want the police to catch the thief. Everyone in Chinatown realized how valuable the Jade Princess was to the Chin family.

Sue was sad. The New Year's celebration would not be the same without the statue in the window of Mr. Chin's shop. The Jade Princess was a sign of happiness.

With a last look at the empty box, the two girls walked away. Sue was quiet for a long time. But she couldn't forget poor Mr. Chin lying on the floor, tied and gagged. She couldn't forget how scared he looked.

Finally she said, "If Mr. Chin won't let us call the police, then we have to help him get the Princess back."

Jenny looked at her with a surprised expression. "Us? How can we do that?"

"I don't know," Sue said. "But we've got to try!"

CHAPTER 4

Sue thought about Mr. Chin and the missing Jade Princess the next day. After school she and Jenny hurried to Mr. Chin's gift shop on Lotus Street.

The Princess of Happiness was not in the window, and the carved ivory box was gone too. But the shop was open for business. Sue and Jenny hurried inside.

Ruth Chin was dusting some pretty painted boxes in a glass cabinet. She smiled when she saw the girls.

"Hello," Ruth said. "I'm glad you stopped by. I want to thank you for helping us yesterday."

Sue looked around, but she did not see Mr. Chin. "Is your father all right?" she asked.

"He's feeling much better today," Ruth said.

Sue was glad to hear that Mr. Chin was all right, but she was still worried about the statue. "Did your father tell you what happened to the Jade Princess?" she asked.

Ruth slowly looked away. She looked sad. In a low, unsteady voice she said, "My father sold it to a friend from China." Ruth closed the cabinet and turned the key in the lock. Then she walked to the front of the shop.

Sue didn't believe what Ruth said. Mr. Chin would never sell the Princess of Happiness! Many people wanted to buy it. They offered a lot of money for it, but Mr. Chin always said that it was not for sale. He said that the Jade Princess belonged to all the people of Chinatown.

"Will your father's friend take the statue back to China?" Jenny asked. She was unable to hide her disappointment.

"Yes." Ruth tried to smile, but she looked ready to cry. She picked up a package from the desk. "I can't go to the Girls' Club today," she said. "Mrs. Smith needs this record. Will you take it to her for me?"

Jenny took the package, then she and Sue left.

Outside, Sue had a worried look on her face. "I think Ruth is hiding something," she said. "She's as scared as her father was yesterday."

Jenny thought so too. "Ruth has never missed dance practice before. If her father is feeling fine, why does she have to work in the shop?"

"Something is going on," Sue said. She glanced back toward the gift shop, then whispered, "Someone was in the back room. I saw the curtain move, and I heard footsteps."

"It was probably Mr. Chin." Jenny said.

Sue didn't think so. She was very curious.

"Come on," she told Jenny. "Let's investigate."

She took Jenny's arm and hurried around the corner. She stopped near the narrow alley that ran behind the shops. She looked both ways to make sure nobody was coming, then she pulled Jenny into the alley.

The narrow space was dark and dirty. There were a lot of trash cans and old boxes. Papers and straw spilled from a big packing box and blew around in a gust of wind. A black and white cat leaped out of a trash can right in front of them. Jenny gasped.

"Shhh!!!" Sue warned. She put a finger to her lips and tiptoed to the rear of Mr. Chin's shop. There was a door and one tiny window that was too high to reach.

Sue looked around and then pointed to a big wooden crate. "Help me move this," she

whispered. They went over to the box.

Jenny lifted one end of the empty box and Sue took the other. They quietly carried it behind Mr. Chin's shop and put it under the window. Sue climbed up on it and peered through the dusty window.

She was looking into the back room of the shop. Ruth was standing near the curtained doorway, talking to someone. The man was standing with his back to the window. Sue did not see his face, but she knew it wasn't Mr. Chin. She stood on her tiptoes and stretched. She wanted to know who the man was. He might have been the one who was scaring Ruth and her father.

Sue stretched as far as she could, trying to see the man's face.

"Watch out!" Jenny suddenly whispered.

But it was too late! The wooden box tipped and one of the boards broke with a loud noise. Sue almost toppled off. She grabbed the edge of the window just in time.

Inside the shop the man heard the noise and turned around. He walked toward the back door. Sue ducked so he could not see her. She scrambled off the box as fast as she could. He was coming out!

Sue grabbed Jenny's hand as they heard the man unlock the door. There wasn't time to get away! Quickly Sue pulled Jenny into another dark doorway, and they pressed themselves back into the shadows.

They held their breath as the door of Mr. Chin's shop opened.

CHAPTER 5

Jenny was shivering. She was too scared to move. Sue put a finger to her lips, warning Jenny to be quiet.

They heard Ruth's voice a short distance away, "There's no one here."

A man's voice answered. "I know I heard something."

Sue and Jenny were very still as they heard the man walking around the alley. Papers rustled. A box scraped on the pavement.

"It was probably only a cat," Ruth said.

Instead of answering, the man walked toward the doorway where Sue and Jenny were hiding. Jenny pressed a hand against her mouth so she would not scream. Just before the man reached the doorway, he stopped and listened. A soft noise came from one of the boxes across the dirty alley. He walked toward it slowly. Then he quickly lifted his foot and kicked the box.

The black and white cat leaped out of the box and jumped onto the fence. It stood there with its back arched and its fur standing on end. The frightened cat spat and yowled.

The man turned angrily and went back to Mr.

Chin's shop. He looked very mean.

"Dumb cat!" he muttered.

Ruth Chin said, "I told you no one was here."

"It's a good thing for you no one is," the man said in a mean voice. "You had better play it smart and not tell anyone about our visit."

"I promise I won't," Ruth said, sounding terribly upset.

"You'd better not, if you know what's good for you!" the man said.

The door squeaked, then slammed. The alley was quiet.

After a moment Sue poked her head out and looked toward Mr. Chin's shop. Ruth and the man were gone, and the door of the gift shop was closed.

"Did you see who that was?" she asked Jenny.

Jenny shook her head. "I was too scared. Come on, let's get out of here before he comes back!"

"It was the fat man who was talking to Mr. Chin in front of the shop yesterday," Sue said.

"Maybe he's Mr. Chin's friend from China."

"He didn't sound very friendly," Sue said. "He made Mr. Chin angry yesterday, and he wasn't nice to Ruth today." She looked at the closed door of the shop. "I think he forced Mr. Chin to sell him the Jade Princess."

"That's silly," Jenny said.

"Or he stole it!" Sue said.

Jenny frowned. "Do you think he was the one who tied up Mr. Chin?"

"Yes, or he had his pal do it for him," Sue said.

"You mean the skinny man who told Mr. Chin he'd be sorry?" Jenny shivered as she remembered how angry the two men were when Mr. Chin threw them out of the shop.

"I think they're working together," Sue said. "Mr. Chin didn't sell them the Jade Princess, so they tied him up and took it."

"Why did they come back today?" Jenny asked.

"To steal more of his treasures," Sue said.

She was sure the men were crooks. "And they'll get away with it if we don't stop them."

Jenny was not as brave as Sue. She didn't want to see the two men ever again. "But what can we do?" she asked.

"We can watch the shop to see when they come out!" Without waiting for an answer, Sue ran to the corner and peered around. Just as she expected, the two men came out after a few minutes. They walked across the street to where the blue car was parked. The fat man opened the car door. He turned and said something in a low voice to the skinny man. Then he got in the car and drove away. The other man shoved his hands in his pockets and whistled as he walked down the street.

"Come on," Sue said quickly. "Let's follow him. We have to find out who he is and where he goes."

Jenny shook her head. "I don't like that idea. We can get in a lot of trouble playing detective!"

"Then I'll go alone!" Sue said as she started after the man.

Jenny stood for a moment. She didn't want to get in trouble, but she couldn't let Sue walk into danger alone.

"Wait!" she called at last. "I'll come with you." She ran to catch up with Sue.

CHAPTER 6

Sue and Jenny stayed half a block behind the skinny man. He stopped at the next corner and looked around while he waited for the traffic light to change. Sue and Jenny had just enough time to turn and pretend they were looking at dresses in a shop window.

After a minute Sue peeked over her shoulder. The skinny man was crossing the street.

"That was a close call," she said. "Come on, he is on his way again."

Jenny wanted to forget the whole thing, but she tagged along after Sue. Sometimes they had to walk more slowly to stay far enough behind so that they wouldn't be seen. They got closer when there were a lot of people around so they would not lose him in the crowd. He was heading for the center of Chinatown.

On Prince Street the man stopped to talk to an old woman standing in the doorway of a basket shop. Sue and Jenny hid behind the big, golden dragon outside the Moon Garden Restaurant. They could see the man, but they could not hear what he was saying. Finally the old woman reached into the pocket of her dress

and took out some money. The skinny man grabbed it out of her hand and slipped it into his jacket. Then he walked across the street and went into a tailor shop.

Sue and Jenny stayed in their hiding place to watch. When he came out, they followed him again.

He walked slowly up and down the streets for a while. He stopped to talk to several people, and he went into two more shops. At Mr. Choy's laundry, Sue was sure she saw him give the skinny man some money. But when he came out of the shop, his hands were empty. He whistled as he walked away.

"We're wasting our time," Jenny said. "He's not doing anything wrong. He's just walking around talking to people."

"But they're giving him money," Sue said.

"Maybe he did some work for them." There were lots of reasons people might give the man money.

Sue was still watching the man. She was sure he was up to something. She wanted to find out where he was going.

Jenny remembered the package Ruth had given her. "We're supposed to be at the Girls' Club now. We're late!"

Sue had forgotten all about dance practice and the package for Mrs. Smith.

"Let's give up," Jenny begged. She didn't like the idea of following a dangerous-looking stranger around Chinatown.

"Just a little while longer," Sue said. She pointed as the man went around a corner. "Hurry, or we'll lose him!" She quickened her steps and Jenny ran to catch up.

Halfway down the block, the tall, skinny man went into a building. As soon as he was out of sight, Sue ran and looked at the sign over the door.

It read: CHINATOWN MEN'S CLUB.

Jenny sighed. "The Men's Club! Everyone in

Chinatown comes here to help with the New Year's parade!"

Sue was disappointed. There was nothing mysterious about the Men's Club. But she still believed the skinny man and his fat friend had stolen the Jade Princess. Perhaps he was robbing other people too. She was not going to give up trying to solve the mystery now.

They heard voices and hammering inside the Men's Club. This was where the big dragon was kept until the night of the grand parade. It was where Jimmy and the other boys practiced carrying it to make it weave and dance. The

Men's Club also did other things for the New Year's celebration. The men made the paper dragon to collect gifts from the shops. Boys and girls in the band practiced their music and marching in the club. Stores and businesses decorated floats with colored paper, ribbons, and flowers.

The Men's Club was a very busy place before the New Year. Sue's brother came every day, and her father did too. Jenny was right. Everyone in Chinatown came to the Men's Club.

Sue was still staring at the door when it opened suddenly. Someone came out and almost bumped into her. It was the tall, skinny man they were following!

He looked at Sue and Jenny. "What are you doing here?" he said in a harsh voice.

Sue and Jenny were too scared to answer.

The man took a step toward them. "You have been following me!" he said. "I saw you near the Moon Garden Restaurant. And I saw you near Mr. Choy's laundry. Now you're here. I don't like to be followed and I don't like snoopy kids! If I catch you following me again, you're going to be in a lot of trouble! Do you understand?"

He raised a fist and shook it at them.

CHAPTER 7

Jenny almost dropped the package of records. She grabbed Sue's arm tightly and got ready to run. She was frightened by the way the man looked at them. He was angry, and he looked dangerous.

Sue didn't feel very brave either, but she forced herself to answer. "We're not following you. I'm looking for my brother."

The man frowned. The expression on his face showed that he didn't believe her. He started to say something just as the door of the Men's Club opened quickly. Two boys came out, talking and laughing.

Sue knew one of them. He was Pete, one of her brother's friends.

Pete smiled. "Hi, Sue. If you're looking for Jimmy, he went over to the school."

"Thanks, Pete. I am looking for him." Sue turned to Jenny and said in a loud voice, "We might as well go, if Jimmy isn't here."

The man standing in the doorway rubbed his chin and looked at her without saying anything.

As she and Jenny walked away, Sue knew that the man was still watching them, but he

didn't follow. At the corner Sue glanced back and saw him walking the other way.

Jenny was shaking. "I told you it was dangerous for us to follow him!" she said.

"At least we have a lead now," Sue said.

"What do you mean, a lead?"

"We're not the only ones who have seen him. Pete and his friend did too."

"What good will that do?" Jenny asked.

"I'll have my brother ask Pete who the man is, and we'll have a clue to his identity."

Jenny shook her head. "I don't think Pete knows him. They didn't say hello."

"But Pete *did* see him," Sue insisted. "And other people in the Men's Club did too. If Jimmy asks around, someone will know who he is."

Jenny wasn't sure she wanted to know. She remembered what the man said about getting in trouble if they didn't stay away from him.

But she knew that Sue was not going to give up.

That night Sue listened to her family talk about the New Year's celebration. It was only two days away! Everyone was getting ready for it. Sue's mother was cooking special New Year's cakes for the holiday. Her grandmother unpacked the small lacquered trunk she kept in her closet. She carefully took out the beautiful old silken robes that Sue and Jenny were going to wear in the dance program. She ironed them carefully and hung them in the closet.

At dinner Sue's father talked about the work everyone was doing to get ready for the parade. Then he frowned.

"It is very odd, but Mr. Chin was not at the Men's Club today. Something strange is going on." He looked around at his family. "Do you know that the Jade Princess is not in Chin's shop window? Everyone in Chinatown is talking about it."

Sue almost dropped her chopsticks. She wanted to ask a million questions, but she stared at her plate and said nothing.

She did not have a chance to talk to Jimmy alone until later when they were in the kitchen, doing the dishes.

Sue asked, "Have there been any strangers at the Men's Club lately?"

Jimmy made a face. "Lots of people come to

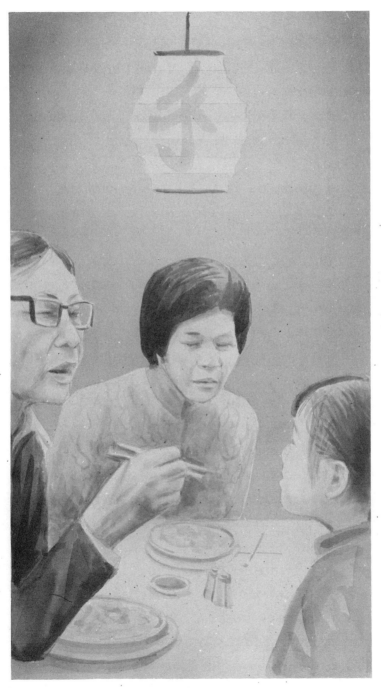

the club this time of year. I don't know them all."

Sue described the tall, skinny man.

Jimmy shook his head. "I don't know him," he said.

"Can you find out who he is?" Sue asked.

Jimmy looked at his sister. "Why do you want to know?"

Sue promised Ruth Chin she wouldn't talk about the missing Jade Princess or the trouble at Mr. Chin's shop. She couldn't break that promise, so she couldn't tell Jimmy why she was asking questions about the strange man.

"I just want to know," she said. "It's important."

Jimmy looked at her with a curious expression. "All right, I'll see what I can find out," he said. "But I hope you aren't getting into trouble. Sometimes you're too snoopy for your own good."

The skinny man said that she was snoopy too! Sue smiled at her brother. "Thanks, Jimmy. I won't get into any trouble. But if I do, I'll yell for you to rescue me."

"That's what big brothers are for," Jimmy teased. "Now let's get these dishes done. I've got to go back to the Club to practice tonight. Did you hear that I'm going to carry the head of the dragon?"

"How lucky can you get? Make sure you don't drop it," Sue teased Jimmy back. Sue was very proud of him, because carrying the dragon's head was the hardest job in the parade.

Jimmy swung the dish towel at her and grinned. "Get busy washing those dishes and quit talking so much."

CHAPTER 8

The next day Sue thought about the Jade Princess and the strange men in Mr. Chin's shop. But she did not have time to talk to Jenny about the mystery. At school their class decorated the room where a New Year's party would be held after the parade. They put up paper lanterns and long ribbons that fluttered like birds. They also put up signs with the Chinese New Year greeting: GUNG HAY FAT CHOY.

After school the Girls' Club practiced the dance program again. It was the first time they wore their costumes. Everyone was excited. The pretty silk robes looked like a rainbow of colors. Some girls wore black robes with pictures stitched in bright colors. Other girls wore blue, red, yellow, or green robes. Everyone was very proud, and the girls danced gracefully.

Ruth Chin was there, but she did not say anything about the Jade Princess. She didn't stop to talk to Sue and Jenny at all. She still looked worried. Sue was sure now more than ever that something was wrong.

Sue's father and brother worked late at the

Men's Club, helping to get everything ready for the parade the next night. Sue couldn't wait to talk to her brother. As soon as he came into the house, she pulled him into her room.

"Did you find out anything?" she asked.

Jimmy nodded. "The man's name is David Low. He's new around here. People say he isn't a very nice guy. He has been in a lot of trouble for fighting and stealing. He's been in prison too." Jimmy looked at Sue. "How do you know someone like him?"

"I don't know him," Sue said. Sue did not like to hear such bad news about the man she and Jenny followed. But it made her surer than ever that David Low and the fat man had stolen the Jade Princess.

"Then why are you asking about him?" Jimmy asked.

Sue shrugged. "I saw him around, and I just wondered." She still couldn't break her promise to Ruth, as much as she wanted to tell Jimmy everything.

Jimmy shook his head. "Stay away from David Low. He's trouble — bad trouble!"

Sue did not sleep very well that night. She dreamed about the Jade Princess. She also dreamed about David Low shaking his fist at her and saying, "If I catch you, you're going to be in a lot of trouble!"

The next day was New Year's Eve. Chinatown was full of excitement. There was much to do, and Sue forgot all about her nightmares. After school, Sue, Jenny, and their friends went to the Men's Club. They were going to follow the dragon as it went from shop to shop. This was the day people gave the dragon gifts so he would bring good luck in the

New Year. Everyone knew the money was used to help people in Chinatown. It was fun to watch the fierce-looking dragon gobble up the dollar bills dropped in his mouth. The dragon danced and twisted from one shop to another. Everyone clapped and laughed when the dragon growled and shopkeepers pretended to be afraid.

When the dragon got to Mr. Chin's shop, Ruth was in the doorway. She took down the lettuce and dollar bills tied to the door and dropped them in the dragon's mouth. She smiled at everyone, but she didn't stay to talk. She hurried inside and closed the door.

Sue did not follow the crowd as it moved on to the next shop. She pushed Jenny around the corner.

"Where are we going?" Jenny asked. "I want to watch the dragon."

Sue pointed toward Mr. Chin's shop. "I think

David Low and his pal are inside!"

Jenny was so surprised that her mouth dropped opened. "I didn't see them!"

"Neither did I, but there's the blue car the fat man drives!" Sue pointed to a car parked across the street. It was the same one!

Just then the door of the shop opened and the fat man and David Low came out. Sue pulled Jenny back. The men walked past the place where the girls were hiding, but didn't see them. They were too busy talking.

"Do it tonight during the parade," the fat man said. "And I don't want any mistakes this time."

David Low said, "Don't worry. I'll get everything."

The fat man crossed the street and got into his car. David Low watched the car drive away. Then he walked down the street, whistling.

Before Jenny could stop her, Sue was following him again.

"Don't follow him!" Jenny warned Sue in a whisper. She was afraid that David Low might turn around and see them. "Remember what he said!"

"We can't let Mr. Chin and Ruth lose everything. You heard him say he'd get everything tonight."

Sue walked faster as David Low went across the street and into an alley. She had to find a way to stop him. She was so worried about losing sight of David Low that she rushed into the alley.

David Low was standing right there — waiting for her!

CHAPTER 9

Sue stopped in her tracks. David Low rushed at her. Jenny let out a scared yelp. Sue grabbed her arm and ran out of the alley as David Low began to chase them.

Sue and Jenny raced down the street. When Sue glanced back over her shoulder, David Low was getting closer. Sue tried to run faster, but it was no use. The next moment David Low grabbed her arm. She tried to get away, but he held her tightly.

"I warned you, you snoopy kid!" David Low said with a mean look.

Sue was so scared, she was shaking. David Low's hand was hurting her arm. Quickly Sue lifted her foot and kicked his leg as hard as she could! He yelled in pain and let go. Before he could grab her again, Sue and Jenny were running.

"This way!" Sue shouted. They ran between two buildings and came out onto the next street. Sue looked both ways, then headed for the corner. Jenny was right behind her.

There was a small grocery store on the corner. After a look to make sure David Low did not see them, the girls ran into the store.

It was a very old shop. It had been in
Chinatown for a long time. There were baskets
of dried fruits and Chinese vegetables. There
were bins of spices and candies from China. A
large wooden box was filled with dried fish.
The store smelled like a hundred different
things.

Sue and Jenny hid behind a tall stack of baskets. Sue peeked out. She saw David Low through the big window. He was standing on the corner looking up and down the street. He didn't know where they had gone. The trick was working!

Behind the counter the owner, Mr. Lee,

smiled and said, "Can I help you?"

Sue dug into her pocket and took out a dime.
"I'd like a box of rice candy, please."

Mr. Lee reached into a glass cabinet and

took out a pink box of candy. He gave it to Sue. As she paid him, she glanced out the window again. David Low was slowly walking away from the store. They were safe!

Sue unwrapped the candy. She gave Jenny a piece, and she popped a piece in her own mouth. She wanted to be sure David Low was far away before they left Mr. Lee's shop. She did not want him to catch them again. Her arm still hurt where he had grabbed her.

"What are we going to do now?" Jenny whispered.

Sue waited until they were outside before she answered. "We can't let him steal all Mr. Chin's things. We are going to stop him."

"How?" Jenny was shaking. She did not ever want to see David Low again!

"I don't know yet," Sue said. "But I am sure he stole the Jade Princess. Now he wants to finish robbing Mr. Chin's shop during the parade tonight."

"We can't go after him alone," Jenny said. "If he sees us again, he is not going to like it."

"I will watch Mr. Chin's shop during the parade," Sue said. "If I see David Low or the fat man go in, I will yell for help until somebody comes!"

As soon as it was dark, people gathered on the street to wait for the parade to begin.

Everyone in Chinatown came. People from other parts of the city came too. The Chinese New Year was one of the biggest celebrations anywhere.

Men and children tossed firecrackers. The noise was supposed to scare away any evil spirits.

The main street of Chinatown was blocked off with ropes and boards. Cars could not go on it. The parade would march right down the middle of the street for everyone to see.

Sue and Jenny picked a spot where they could see the parade. From there they could see Mr. Chin's shop. There was no sign of David Low or the fat man, but Sue was sure they were going to come.

Finally the parade began. Music, shouting, and laughter filled the air. The first marchers came along. They stepped in time to music played by the high school band. Two girls dressed in red and blue costumes led the way. They were twirling and tossing batons into the air.

Next the New Year's Queen of Chinatown came by in a shiny black car with the top down. She wore a long white dress and carried red roses in her arms. She smiled and waved at everyone, and she threw pieces of candy wrapped in paper to the children.

Another band marched by. Then there was a
shout. "The dragon is coming!"

CHAPTER 10

Sue stood on tiptoes. With so many interesting things to see, she forgot about watching Mr. Chin's shop. She wanted to see the dragon most of all because Jimmy was helping to carry it.

The dragon's tail was held up by 10 boys. Their heads were hidden under the dragon's long, paper body. The dragon had a fierce face. It had painted eyes, with bright colored feathers all around them. Its big mouth was open, to show long teeth and a red tongue. Red and yellow ribbons made it look as if the dragon were breathing fire.

Jimmy danced from side to side, making the dragon chase people. Children screamed and threw fireworks in front of him. When Jimmy shook the dragon's head and roared, people yelled.

Just as the dragon reached the spot where Sue and Jenny were standing, Sue remembered the missing Jade Princess. She turned to look at Mr. Chin's shop. She looked just in time. David Low was coming out the door. He had a large package under his arm. He looked around, then hurried toward the street.

Mr. Chin ran out of the shop. "Stop, thief!" he yelled. He pointed to David Low, who ducked into the crowd.

Sue went after David Low. "Stop that man!" she yelled. "Come on, Jenny!" Jenny followed Sue, but everyone else was too busy watching the dragon to notice.

David Low shoved past people and headed toward the corner. When Sue and Jenny looked, they saw the blue car parked on a side street. The fat man was waiting for Low. If he reached the car, they would both get away. Then Mr. Chin's treasures would be gone!

Sue ran through the crowd. People were laughing and shouting as the dragon came close. She pushed her way to the curb and tried to get Jimmy's attention. He saw her and began to tease. He pushed the dragon's fierce face down and pretended to bite her.

Sue pointed at David Low and shouted over the noise of the crowd. "David Low robbed Mr. Chin! He's getting away! We have to stop him!"

Suddenly the dragon's head rose above the crowd. Jimmy looked out. He saw the man running away. In a flash he changed the dragon's direction. The boys carrying the dragon's tail were surprised, but they followed Jimmy. The dragon raced along the street.

David Low saw the dragon coming after him.

He tried to duck into the crowd. But the dragon's head swooped down at him. Jimmy's foot shot out and tripped him. Low sprawled on the sidewalk.

Sue and Jenny ran up to him. Quickly, Sue grabbed the package from under his arm. Low tried to get it back, but the dragon kept poking at him. People hurried over to see what was going on.

"This man is stealing Mr. Chin's treasures!" Sue told them. Sue heard a car start. She looked up and saw the blue car pulling away from the curb.

"That's his partner!" she yelled. "Don't let him get away!"

At that moment several policemen ran out a door and stopped the car. They made the fat man get out, and they brought him back to the crowd.

Sue held up the package. "They were trying to steal Mr. Chin's treasures," she said.

One of the policemen took the package and opened it. Inside was a stack of papers.

Sue and Jenny did not believe their eyes. Sue was sure David Low and the fat man had stolen valuable art treasures. But these were only papers! Everyone was looking at Sue. She felt very foolish.

Just then Mr. Chin and Ruth rushed up. "Thank you for stopping this man," Mr. Chin said to Sue. "You are both very brave girls."

Sue was confused.

"What's going on?" Jimmy asked.

Mr. Chin said, "These papers have the names and addresses of new people who come to Chinatown. They belong to the Men's Club. David Low and his partner, Sam, are extortionists. They pretend to work for the government. They tell people that they will be sent back to China if they don't pay them money. They believe Low and Sam, and pay the money." Mr. Chin looked at the two men and frowned. "Low and Sam wanted my lists to blackmail more people. I chased them away, but they kept coming back."

Sue was amazed. "What about the Jade Princess? If Low and Sam didn't steal it, where is it?"

Ruth said, "My father took it out of the window because he knew they would try to steal it. He hid the statue, but when David Low and Sam came back, they tied him up and searched the shop. They know how much the Jade Princess means to my father and the people of Chinatown. They said they wouldn't return it unless he gave them what they wanted." Ruth smiled at her father.

"But my father loves the people of Chinatown even more than he does the Jade Princess. He would never betray them. He called the police and laid a trap for Low and Sam. When they came back tonight, Low threatened to burn

90

down the shop with us in it. My father gave
him the papers, but he knew the police were
watching Sam's car."

The policemen put handcuffs on David Low

and Sam. Then they searched the blue car.
They found the Jade Princess in the trunk. They
handed it to Mr. Chin.

Mr. Chin smiled as he looked around at the

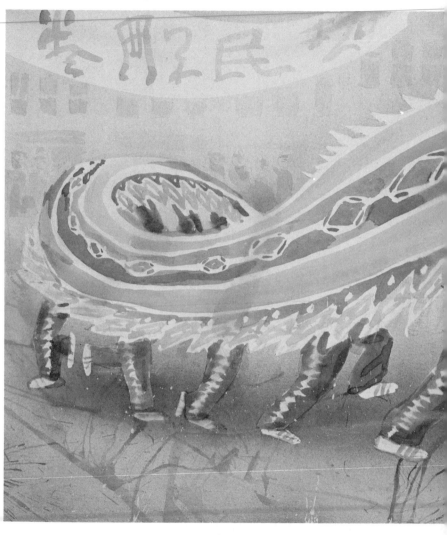

crowd. "Sue and her friend Jenny have helped a lot of people today. And they have saved the Jade Princess!"

Sue and Jenny blushed. Then Sue said, "It was Jimmy who came to the rescue."

"That's what big brothers are for," Jimmy teased. "Now let's get on with the parade. Sue,

will you help me carry the dragon's head? I could use a brave helper." Jimmy grinned as he raised the fierce head into the air.

The music began. Jimmy, Sue, and Jenny danced down the street. Sue was very happy. With the Jade Princess smiling on Chinatown again, this was the best New Year ever!

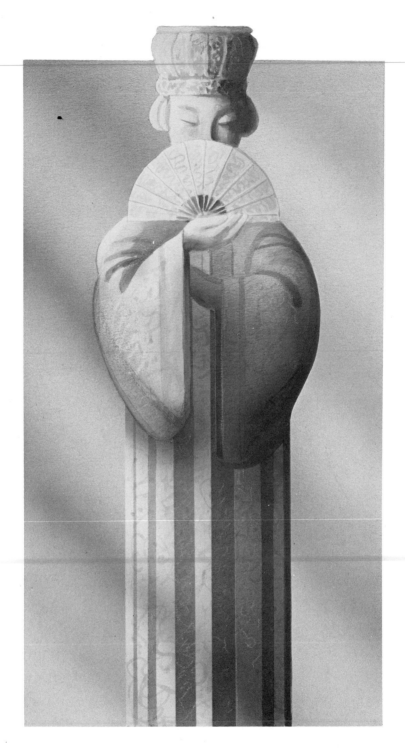